Mindful Cornucopia

Nigel Derbyshire

Carbon Writer

Carbon Writer 2019

Mindful Cornucopia
by Nigel Derbyshire

First Edition: January 2019

ISBN 978-1-9164156-6-9

Publisher
Carbon Writer
carbonwriter.net
publisher@carbonwriter.net

Dedication

For my wonderful kids, Amy & Oliver.

Acknowledgements

We wander into all sorts of people in our lives, sometimes they turn out to be nasty, and sometimes not. Here are a few from the latter;

Amy & Oliver, for just being lovely kids & making me proud.

Nicky Derbyshire, for being sensible throughout.

Jo Polley, for helping me to see a new version of my future.

Daisy Blue, for being an unexpected muse.

Marie, for helping me with my junk.

Jules Watson, Liz Wade, Stewart Barrett, Ian Gardner, all for reminding me what old friends look like.

My Sister Andrea, for all the years of teasing and laughter.

My Mum, for keeping me safe and loving me unconditionally.

Preface

I'm not quite sure what you are expecting to read here, but I can tell you that you are probably going to be wrong.

Lets not go into why you are wrong, and lets also be clear that I am not right.

My attempt here is to provide some thinking matter for you. Not in a bold pretentious kind of way, but in an undefined way that is hopefully accessible. Yeah, I don't like that word "accessible" either.

I'm not going to insult your intelligence, or make a statement around the lack of it.

What we have here is a collection of musings that have wandered out of my brain, and which I have attempted to capture; a range of topics.

I do not claim to be smarter than anyone else, just a person who needs to express the inner workings of his mind. I guess that in itself says something about me.

There are 2 different types of content to expect here; articles and poetry. The Musings are just that, and are thoughts that I found kicking around in my head, which I then decided to write down. The Poetry is free verse in style, and often quite dense. For those pieces of work, I have added a short note at the start of each one so you can get an insight into what I was attempting.

There is no correct way to approach this book; feel free to skip the Musings and go straight to the Poetic work, or just open a random page.

You have permission to scribble in the margins; I would love to see any that you make - send me a photo!

I hope you can get something from reading my work, as I certainly got something in writing it.

Feel free to connect with me, either via twitter @carbonwriter, or email nigel@carbonwriter.net, if you have any comments, observations, or just want to say hello.

Nigel,

January 2019.

nigelderbyshire.com

Musings

Poetry

Closing

Musings

A gentle stroll down the ambling lane of my musings.

Why do we write things down?

I have been wondering about this for a while now, and I think there are a number of reasons.

If I have a list of things to do, or items to get, that is longer than 2, then I write it down.

1. Eggs

2. Cheese

3. Bread

While I could probably remember these items, I choose to free up that little bit of brain power. Instead I simply need to remember one thing.

1. Where is the list?

So I have simplified the problem; a reason to write something down. As an organisational shortcut or tool.

There is also a laziness angle here too. If I write it down then I don't have to bother reorganising my brain to remember the list. As someone who does not have a magic list-creating mind, the process of remember a sequence of items requires a certain amount of effort. To be honest, I just can't be bothered.

Walk around a supermarket and look at the number of people with lists. On one level you could very rationally think that they are super organised individuals who have taken the time to carefully curate and create a list of items. I get more joy out of thinking of them as just plain lazy.

Writing something down does have one advantage over the act of just remembering it. It is a hard-backup.

Your brain has a wonderfully magical way of self-reorganisation. It is always trying to do different things, it is never still, always trying to be better. Now it has to be said that my version of "better" is different from yours, and I know that my mind can massively cock things up in trying to be "better".

In brain-reorg-mode there can, on occasion, be some "collateral damage".

I'm sure you have experienced it, you know, when that list of shopping that you absolutely must get on your way home, gets partially overwritten by the colour of your favourite pants when you were 5 years old. There is no warning of this either. There is no flashing amber triangle against the start of that list, saying that it might have been accidentally trashed. As you walk down isle 13 feeling slightly smug that you have so far managed to retrieve 6 items from the list, you suddenly find yourself thinking about the colour red...

An off-brain backup serves a valuable purpose, in it's purity and rigid nature.

Sharing content is another reason that we write things down. Instructions on how to get somewhere, or a verse of poetry that you found. All good things to share with others, and the written word is perfect for this. It is not subject to the brain-reog-mode effect, and is portable. The unit of writing can be easily transported to the desired party.

An additional bonus item here, is that it does not change on its own accord; the information remains the same. Sure someone can pro-actively modify it, but that requires positive action and intent. Without those two, the writing will not change itself.

There is a curious edge-case though; stories.

There is a mixed tradition here, it would seem; story-reading and story-telling. The former is massively popular and is used by all and sundry as a mechanism of escapism. Of running a movie in your head that is crafted for you, where you are the camera operator. With only you and the written word, and a possibly complex story, it needs to work. If you as a reader get lost, then you may wander away.

Story-telling is different. There is an actor-presenter of the story, and there is the audience. There is an interaction between the two, and our brains seems to relish interactions. The subtle and not so subtle connection between the two, feeds into the brain's reorg-mode in real time. The story gets "edited" in real-time; in pacing, in scope, in content. There also seems to be a post-performance editing that goes on too, so that the next time small changes are made to make the story "better".

This can of course be dangerous, the in-head editing can sometimes go too far. Jumping from a bridge that is 60 feet high, that changes into 65 feet on the next telling, that changes to 7 stories high, is ok. Extending that to 100 feet next telling is just too far. Thankfully the reality feedback loop can fix that.

The written story-book does not have that feedback loop, so has to remain the same. Which is actually a good thing, for readers.

So far, I hope that all of these reasons that we write things down have made a kind of sense. We write things down as a tool, as a form of entertainment, as an item of record. There is another reason though, and for me this is the most important reason.

For some people, me being one, my brain is a free-wheeling-hyperbowling-editing-rewriting-overthinking-massive-powerhouse-loud-noisy-machine. Or FWHEROMPLNM for short; society has put a label on it, but I'm ignoring that and using that piece of freed up brain to remember that I like the colour blue.

What does that mean? This is my personal view, but it might illustrate my point.

Imagine that you are standing on the edge of a motorway / freeway / autobahn, looking straight ahead across the traffic. The traffic is racing by quickly. It is noisy and blustery. You can see the blur of the traffic, you can hear the orchestra of them. In some sense the blur is colourful and the sound is hypnotic. In another sense, you have a requirement to pick out all of the blue cars, or to cross to the other side, or to count the number of cars that have more then one passenger. The louder the noise, the greater the traffic, the harder the task, the more important the task.

Still with me?

I find that writing things down, or more specifically creating written content, has the rather curious effect of either slowing the traffic down, or reducing the amount of traffic, or lessening the noise. It is almost as if it is emptying my brain a little and giving it magical extra capacity.

What am I saying?

The "process" of writing is internally beneficial. The way in which you need to assemble your thoughts in to a line, straight or curvy; the mechanical action of outputting that into or onto something; the hard-backup that is created. It all helps. It feels as if the words and content have been let free from their cage. From a cage that would continuously overthink it, from a cage that would continuously re-edit it, from a cage that was surrounded with other cages that were all bumping against each other.

I believe that the main reason, the most important reason that we write, is for the benefit of one's self, and the effect on others is just a useful side effect.

Nigel Derbyshire

The balance and relative importance of those two benefits, self vs others, differs for each person. For myself, I initially started writing because I wanted other people to read it. That has now completely changed. I now write for myself. Not in a selfish negative way, but in a self-preservation kind of way.

I think writing is important. What do you think?

Good Enough is all we need; semi-colons are proof that is wrong

The existence of the semi-colon is proof that "Good Enough" just isn't.

As I go through life, sometimes running, sometimes sitting, sometimes falling, sometimes climbing, there is a sense that you just need to do "Enough". There is that underlying trend that whilst you need to do your best, it is also perfectly OK to do "enough".

Generally I have found that this is linked to the idea that life is full of destinations. It is full of places to get to, either physically, emotionally, or mentally. It is a series of points. Get to and through them, and you are making progress. Granted, sometimes we go backwards, but that is OK too. You just need to know where the next point is, and head towards it.

Look at the modern techie world, and you see that people are executing on this big time. They are rushing to the next point, the next tweet, the next snapchat thing, the next high score. A massive series of points that need to be visited and ticked off.

In 1494 Italian printer Aldus Manutius created the semicolon, with Ben Jonson being the first English writer to use it systematically decades later. It can be used to link related clauses. It can also be thought of as a longer pause than a comma, but not quite a full stop. You don't have to use it at all. It is not like a full stop, that always needs to be used. It is not like a comma, which you can use to add some pause and tone to the written sentence; it is something different.

The semi-colon is something that doesn't really need to exist. Its usage has also declined in recent decades too, from the peak in the 1800s, but it is still around today.

In a world of destinations, in a world of full-stops and commas, what does the semi-colon say about it all?

It is a powerful reminder of something so important, that it defines a fundamental human trait. Journey.

There is a tremendous pressure to get to the next point, to get to the next event, to get the next best grades, to be next, or to be first. There is a focus on full-stops. The commas are only there to let you plan, to briefly pause, so that you can get to the next full-stop more efficiently.

The semi-colon doesn't help with any of that. It does nothing but add noise. It is rubbish and has no place here. It is still here though, you see it kicking around sometimes. So, why am I talking about this?

The semi-colon reminds us that the word-journey and sentence landscape is just as important as the concluding marks. In fact, you can't just throw a semi-colon into a sentence, like you can with a comma; thought is needed.

You need to plan for a semi-colon, you need to appreciate the sentence, the tone and the style. It needs to be worked into the sentence to make it work. Adding a semi-colon can elevate a mundane sentence into something special; semi-colons add value.

Semi-colons teach us that for some the journey of a sentence is just as important as the contents of the sentence, and more important than the destination.

We still use them now, some 500 years later. How has something that is 'odd' still managed to stick around? Could it be that the it is an example that shows that, although we are currently focused on commas and full-stops, that we are at heart more of a journey people.

Despite what we are currently being programmed for, at our core we are all about the journey.

Travel defines us as a race, and the semi-colon is the literary from of that.

OK, what does this have to do with "enough"? In truth, it probably has nothing to do with just doing enough, but here you have proof that "enough" is trivial; you have just followed a word journey this far on the promise that I will explain the value of the semi-colon.

I can hear the swans fighting

Sometimes there are things that are just difficult to handle. They are difficult to handle either because of the 'difficult' bit or the 'handle' bit.

There are days when I am presented with complicated and difficult problems, that I just breeze through. No problem at all.

There are other days where I am presented with normal everyday problems that I just can't process at all. It is not related to the problem itself, but rather to my ability to handle it. In a sense it feels like I don't have the tools to deal with it.

The tools I'm referring to, are the ones that we carry around in our heads. We use them every single day, and mostly without even having to think about them. It's a bit like riding a bike, once you have mastered those tools and skills then, it just happens.

There are a group of tools that live in all of our heads that, when presented with a problem, they do a number of things.

1. Assess the problem quickly.

2. Determine if the problem needs to be solved.

3. Creates a super-quick viability assessment of it; is it likely to be solvable?

4. Choose the correct problem-solving tools for the problem.

5. Start the solving process.

6. (In the case of good problem solvers) Loop back to the beginning and repeat.

This pattern happens to us all, and all the time.

Lets look at each one of those items, for a moment.

Assess the problem quickly

The key points here are 'problem' and 'quickly'. Before we even get started we need to look at the 'thing' and determine and recognise that it is actually a problem, and we need to do that quickly.

In some cases this is an instinctive process. For example, if you are driving a car and see a road sign telling you of a sharp corner ahead, then the 'problem' is your 'speed' and if it needs to be adjusted. This needs to be done, and it needs to be done quickly. If it is not, then the nature of the problem will certainly change.

In other cases, the identification of the problem is a little more complex. If you see someone crying, is that a problem? Well, it would depend on the setting. There is a difference between someone crying having just opened a letter, and someone crying at the movies while watching a film. So, the context is also important.

Context also extends to the first example too; you can see the road sign telling you of a sharp corner ahead, but if you have the context of a passenger then that changes the problem.

All of this has to happen quickly. If it does not, then the nature of the problem could change. So it needs to happen quickly to give the next stages the best chance.

Determine if the problem needs to be solved

There are problems, and then there are problems that need to be solved by you. It is perhaps the last part, 'by you', that is the key here.

Taking another look at the sharp corner, if you are the driver of the car then it is certainly something that needs to be 'solved'; if you are a passenger, then it still needs to be solved, just not by you.

This can get complicated though. Take for a moment the person crying. We have already introduced the notion of context as being important, and in that example it was more about the situation or location of the event. What about if the person crying at the movies was your significant other? What if that person opening the letter was a complete stranger, but who was sitting on their own in a cafe?

These complexities are where most of us can get ourselves into trouble. There is an internal conflict between wanting to help, needing to help, and having to help. The context of the situation will add weight to each of those urges, but our own historical experiences also add weight too. If you too have received a break-up letter from some-one and have cried your heart out in a cafe, you will know the utter despair and rejection that causes. So you may consider a kind word or two to the person in the cafe crying over a letter they have just opened. Conversely, you may have also experienced the intensely private grief of reading of a loved one's death in a letter, where personal space is important, so you may just pay for their bill as you leave.

It is this area that most people struggle with, as the number of inputs required to allow for it to happen are many and varied. Life experience and context being the most important.

Is it likely to be solvable?

This doesn't get any easier, does it?

OK, so the solvability of a problem has a feed-back into the amount of effort you are likely to put into it. Perceived easy problems will get 'solved' quickly. There is another context problem here too, though. What do you define as 'sol-ved'?

The future perception of the solution is a major factor here. This is still an instinctive view, but it does feedback into the process and does again tend to be different for different people. For some, getting the person to stop crying is the solution, for other it's just a warm glance so that they know someone else has been there too. In either case, the possibility of a solution of some kind is a key drive into whether the problem progresses.

Having said that, for some the very notion that the problem appears to be unsolvable, is a tremendous driver to them pursuing it. This anti-solving approach would seem to suggest that they like the actual problem-solving process above the problem resolution.

This initial instinctive view of the problem resolution, clearly has an experience element to it too. If you have solved a similar problem in the past, then you are more likely to know that you can solve it in the future and indeed present.

If this initial scoping and assessment takes too long, then there is a distinct danger that the problem will change, and so the whole exercise will be flawed.

Correct problem solving tools

The final pre-solving stage, is the correct selection of tools that you are going to apply to the given problem. This may sound slightly over analytical, but having a notion or an initial plan of attack is what helps you move onto the solving part.

Where you are unsure, it will result in either a hesitation or a sense of self-doubt about your ability.

There can be situations that you know that you have solved in the past, but just can't quite remember how you did it. So, you will arrive at this stage in the process and stall a little. This lack of confidence can be offset by the knowledge that you did it before, but will probably result in an increased level of stress as you progress onto the next stage.

We all have a wide variation of skills we can apply to a given problem, both conscious and subconscious in awareness. Some are physical skill level, while others are knowledge based. For example, it may be that your skill is that you know that the visual problem before you is actually the result of a non-visual problem, so you need to apply some investigative and change of perspective tools to it.

Start solving the problem

Now, assuming that nothing has changed then you can get to work on solving the problem.

There is nothing really extra to say about this, other than it consists of using the tools against the problem, and continuing until the problem is no longer a problem.

The feedback loop

Experience in problem solving will surely demonstrate the importance of always re-assessing the original problem, and then tweaking anything. This loopback ability is often what differentiates between good and poor problem solvers.

The problem solving summary

1. Assess

2. Determine

3. Viability

4. Tools

5. Start

6. Re-check

So, there you have my view of problem solving. I expect you are wondering why I have taken all these words to get to this point. The point, or rather the perspective, that I want to raise is "poor mental health".

As someone who has been given various labels surrounding my own poor mental health, I am struck that for me poor mental health often results in a breakdown of any one of these items.

At various times, I have indeed been unable to see problems that are right in front of me (1). Have got stuck at the Determine (2) stage for so long that the problem has actually changed. Judging Viability (3) becomes particularly challenging, and I will often start trying to solve problems that are either unsolvable or are just not even mine! Tool selection (4) is always a minefield of worrying about selecting the correct method to proceed. Once I am ready to go, sometimes the thought of Starting (5) will cause me to freeze up and stall. Let's not even talk about my ability to Re-check (6).

Other times, I can breeze through problem solving, but when times are bad inside my head, it is this area that is a pretty good barometer as to where I am at.

I mention all of this, not just to give a small insight into the topic, but also as a guide to others. If you see someone you know struggling with solving problems, of all kinds, or just getting stuck at a particular stage, and especially if it is out of character, then please take a moment to think about it.

That moment that you take, the positive caring action that you may undertake, could well have a massively positive effect on the person.

The Edge of Something

The motorway ahead was clear, and I was casually cruising along at a steady 70 mph. I was relaxed and calm.

As I glanced in the rearview mirror, my subconscious tagged something as 'unusual'. Looking again, I could make out a blue smudge approaching, a car. Nothing unusual there, but this car seemed to be closing a little faster than normal.

I checked my speed, yep still doing a steady 70. How fast was he going? An instinctive calculation guessed at close to 100. I moved my head to see if he was being chased, nothing.

I stared into the side mirror, and it wasn't so much the speed that was a surprise, rather the object itself. It looked, for all things, like a rusty old 1980s Eastern-Block Skoda. It was vaguely blue in colour, with patches of brown covering the hood; rust. It didn't have any go faster stripes, or anything like that. No, it just looked normal. Normal except for the immense speed it was traveling at.

The car weaved slightly as I continued to stare.

I expected the driver, who must have been an utter mad-man, to be just that. Either that, or a boy racer type.

As the object became ever closer, I saw a lipstick adorned brunette, of mid-20s. She didn't look, from what I could see, in anyway 'odd', nope she was just driving. She didn't even look as though she was in anyway annoyed, or angry. Nope she just looked 'normal'.

She looked as though she had just decided, in an almost casual way, that she wanted to get from A-to-B a fast as possible, and that would be that.

Her foot must have not just been pressed hard onto the accelerator, it must have been buried into the engine compartment. In fact, it must have been like that for some considerable time.

It wasn't so much the speed, or indeed the un-usual vehicle that was being propelled. No, it was the driver's utter disregard of the limitations of the car she was driving, together with her appar-ent defiance of the laws of physics.

The car was travelling well beyond its factory-new designed limitations. This knackered old car was about to expire, and at that kind of speed it would be both spectator and almost certainly fatal.

As it very briefly drew level and rapidly passed, I felt myself smile. The smile was made up of a curious wonder and joy. It was that kind of feeling you get when you see something not just unusual, but something that shouldn't exist in the first place. It almost felt magical.

The magic was the fact that the driver was so totally unaware of what was about to happen. She wasn't ignorant, or even stupid. She didn't have a death wish. She wasn't racing anyone. She had, in a wonderful mental act of defiance, decided that the limitation of the car weren't a factor and certainly weren't of any concern. By ignoring them, she had excluded them from her version of reality.

The gentle curve of the road ahead provoked the car to pitch to one side, but there wasn't even a flicker of brake lights. At some point soon, perhaps very soon, the car was going to fail. That

moment seemed close, but not quite present.
The magic was in that not-quite-present moment,
my smile broadened into a grin and the magical
shiver trickled down my back.

Poetry

My poetry is best described as dense free verse.

I don't have any preferred topics, but will often write about the differences between my internal perceptions of reality and actual reality.

I do not often *choose* to write something, more that I am *compelled* to write it. I will get this over-whelming need to put something to paper, and I have found that I feel mentally healthier when I give-in to that urge.

I've added some short notes before each piece of work, to give you a fighting chance at under-stand what the heck I was wittering on about.

As a general rule, my work is unedited. That is to say, I believe that when I am writing, there is a di-rect connection between my mind and writing it down. To edit it afterwards, I fear, would be to re-move some of the density of thought. I will cor-rect spelling mistakes, but I will not change capitalisation or how the lines break. When I am writing, I can *feel* the words and their placement, so it would seem a shame to 'fix' that.

My inspiration comes from life, but more specifically the texture of life. There are lots of things to see and to feel, I like the combination of the two. I also suffer from poor mental health, so my sometimes distorted view of reality will often provide another angle to life.

I have taken to annotating each work with the date it was written, this is purely for my own indulgence so I can see how my work changes over time. I guess though, that it does add a little extra piece of meta to the work too.

I hope that you get something from reading my poetry; I got something out of writing it.

Feel free to contact me,

either via twitter (@carbonwriter)

or email (nigel@carbonwriter.net), if you have any comments, observations, or just want to say hello.

Reflection

I was travelling home late one night, on a train. I was tired and day dreaming. As I looked outside the window into the dark night, all I could see was the reflective and slightly distorted reflections of the brightly lit cabin. This alternative distorted but curious reality danced before me.

1-December-2015

Deceive during a glance;
perfect and deformed.

Watch as others look;
a visual fiction.

Tease from the corner of an eye;
a multiplex of content.

Morning throws assist;
at night expose.

Define what I am;
reflect what I have become.

there

During the destruction of a relationship, it was a curious mix of emotions and turmoil. Experiencing the pain, during which I was trying to find some light, I kept falling and failing. At the finality of it all, I realised that the fact that there was a light that I was trying to grasp, was the lesson here. It didn't matter if I managed to grasp it (I did not), but it was the almost magical nature that it existed.

22-April-2018

There is a moment before you are drunk
that is blazing full of light.

There is a moment before you sleep that is
full of wonder.

There is a moment before you smile that is
crammed with optimism.

There is a moment before you die that is full
of your life.

These moments are unique.

These moments are yours.

Savour them, for they lay a path before you
full of gold not yet discovered.

Discovered in mind, but not yet discovered
in this life or reality.
Push it forward, with all your rich complex
heart.
Implore your soul to extract every last ounce
of life from that life-fed gold.

As you stumble and fail.
Fail thinking.
Fail any way that you can.
For it is failing to grasp the new light that is
before you, that makes you realise that,

The light is there.

Nigel Derbyshire

Broken red

Seeing a broken old sofa in a pub, I mused about the stories it could tell. A physical expression of life.

20-February-2018

Bright red, dark rich edges.
Scars of life, random and predictable.
Overly soft, rough inside;

A visual feast of texture and historic love.
History leaving its mark; how many owners?

Polish fails to hide your story.
Love making; arguments; wine, red.
Your unspoken past, betrayed in your texture.

Textured leather of life, presented and inviting.

Familiar location, colour.

Comforting, inviting.

Absorbing new history and memories.

Red leather pub sofa; complete.

88ers

Written for a school reunion, this is a fun folly into my past.

4-September-2018

The brink of the internet;
Unimagined and yet the sense of something
close.

Red brick second block,
Maths, French, German.

Full of stupid teachers,
Who could swim the English Channel,
Speak languages, and teach the universal
Language of mathematics.

White socks for no reason,
Assertion through conflict,
Fuelled via school discos.

Random GCSE text books, for teachers.
Radioactive sheep and
Crushes on teachers.

Ms MacLean for English,
Ms Saunders for Maths.
Innocent fun and not so.

Full of boisterous life,
Normal life.
Running down the school field in the dark,
Hands in pockets; waiting for the halfway
drop.

1988 was its conclusion,
It all started so much further back;

Long may it carefully, with reckless love,
Proceed before us.

The 88.

Nigel Derbyshire

String of life

This talks about the point at which I decided to re-move medication as the main stay of my exist-ence. I could continue along in a medicated mode, but it was starting to have a negative affect on me. I needed to feel empowered and I needed to feel more alive and in control of myself

23-August-2018

The string of myself
Plucked by the cruel.
Covered in medicated soup,
Aggravated; subdued; dulled.

Thick copper strings
Green from exposure
Green from no touch
Sharp, noisy, harsh,
A plague of noise.

Provoked
Painful
Broken?

Mindful Cornucopia

Told of noise,
Helpless but conformed.
Pointless, but medicated Calm.

Enforced Calm,
Enforced Conformity,
Enforced Hope.

Rich Pure Reality
Glimpse into alternative hope.
Hope - Raw - Pure.

Cleaned strings
Removed of soap
Green and sticky
Covered in med-free contact,
Sharp in Noise.

Harsh,
Rubbish,
Complicated.

Pure Self.
Goodness.
Power.

Renewed.

Nigel Derbyshire

Selfie

Written as I looked on at a young couple take selfies, over dinner. Were they inter-acting or just co-acting?

23-August-2018

Spontaneously staged.

Multiple, Curated.

Genuinely Posed.

Conditionally Posted; Shared.

Reviewed; deleted; celebrated.

Night

I have always been curious about the border between night and day. Not dusk, but that moment when it actually turns into night. Things change, and I'm not always sure which I prefer; probably night.

19-July-2018

There is that razor between day and night;
when?

Noon, the sister.
Saccharin,
Bright,
noisy.

Night, dominant.
Slow, deep & black.
Wanting for affection,
Alluring; dangerous.

Holding a diamond handled razor,
gold, sharp blade.
The distorted velvet black noise of invita-
tion.
Intoxicating.

Noon; full of light.
Night; full of taste.

Choose.

Newness

I was in a panic before I wrote this, not knowing what I was going to do next. I found it difficult to see into the future. I knew that I could exist, but I wanted and needed something more. A chance encounter, and now I can see a different future, a future that looks inviting and exciting!

4-September-2018

The dark blue under foot,
Rich and cool, inviting
It roles before me, like
overly generous chocolate.

It warmly caresses my feet,
as I shuffle northwards.

Slightly damp, but familiar.
Slightly firm, but reassuring.

Its rules of engagement are
Invitingly clear;
Keep shuffling; northwards.

Nigel Derbyshire

Northwards, into the cool,
Into the dark,
Into the the...

No, I don't want to shuffle.
I want to run.
I want to run to the...

My feet are bleeding,
the rich blue razor blades,
tearing into them;
Determined to make me shuffle.

A distant warm glow, behind me.
I need it, I need not to be here.

My red feet mashing against the blue.
Looking up, I see a bright orange,
burning my eyes.

Warming my face,
Reaching towards it,
pulling at the orange sky,
all my might, all my energy.

The warm is nearby,
my feet have stopped bleeding.

Surrounded by orange,
distance is blue.

Future Happiness.
New Direction.
Current Newness.

Calm.

Nigel Derbyshire

Burning

Stress is a strange thing, well certainly for me. I can be hyper stressed and in a really nasty place, then out of nowhere it can all disappear... In this case it was a bird song, but sometimes it is just a smile from a stranger, or a good laugh at a corny joke. Stress really is an odd bedfellow.

4-September-2018

The burning stress

Of the stress,

Of the burning,

That burns,

Fuelled by the burning,

Stress;

Extinguished by bird song.

Closing my eyes

When it all gets too much, I have to close my eyes and just breathe.

5-September-2018

I close them and see blue

I close them and feel red

I close them and hear noise

I close them and breathe

I breathe and see nothing

I breathe and feel calm

I breathe and hear music

I open my eyes and feel warmth.

Broken

Having a broken mind is a curious thing. It is both toxic and wonderful. This explores the idea that there is someone who collects broken-ness, at great personal cost and damage, but for the ultimate resolution of the broken; un-broken.

9-September-2018

The collector collects,
reaping on what he has sown;
Rich orchids wrapped in toxic weeds.

Curating the find,
sorting by texture; colour; decay.

The inward delight wrapped in darkness.
Wrapped in the selfish pleasure of owner-
ship.

Collecting broken-ness, owning it.
Collecting broken fragments, decaying,
rusty, discarded & lost, then found.

At his desk, weeds scratching his hands,
Light obscured by the undergrowth,
that has become overgrowth.

Carefully, painfully, pulling at the broken.
Pulling with his hands, his tools.
His eyes dulled by the poor light,
hands discoloured by the dirt.

Then,
with deliberate movement,
with deliberate skill,
with deliberate focus;
extracted.

Extracted; placed; separated.

Broken, carefully, painstakingly,
curated.
The old dirt and pain removed,
absorbed at cost.

Then,
the shiny golden purity, released.
Freedom from the old broken-ness.
Freedom to find new owners.

Nigel Derbyshire

The broken curator;
The forgotten ancient skill;
The cost to release,
The joy of knowledge of newness.

The Un-broken.

Foggy Perspective

A foggy morning from two different perspectives.

5-November-2018

The Fog of the morning.
Thick, wet, forbidding.
Street lights push through,
Yellow dirty light.

The smell of the city.
Artificial and Toxic.

The Fog of the morning.
Thick, wet, alluring.
Ambitious lights, bursting through.
Rich Yellow and optimistic.
The fresh smell of morning,
Pure and divinely new.

Perspective changed.

Nigel Derbyshire

The same thing

*It sometimes takes just as long to start something
as it does to finish something.*

10-November-2018

How long does it take
To finish something Old?

How long does it take
To start something New?

Old verses New,
Just the same
Thing from each end.

Word Salad

My poor mental health sometimes makes constructing sentences rather a challenge. This is about that, and how it feels to me.

10-November-2018

Each word needs a neighbour
A friend who means something,
A path that leads to a destination
To be placed in sequence.

To start and finish the journey
to get there.
To complete the Thought.

What happens if there is no Path?
If there is no destination?
What happens to the words if
There is no sequence to them?

A head full of Word Salad.
Complex, interesting, but lost of form.

More words added, more and more, added.
More noise, more overwhelming colour.
Too much. Too many.

The sky is full of words, everything all at
once.

Falling.

Falling into a pit full of obscenely colourful
words.
Falling into a pit of ever increasing words.

More noise.

The sky is falling in.
Drowning.
Then.
Seeing a tiny new path.

Quickly fill it with words before it is too
much.
A path to a New Thought.

Then,
Repeat, again.

Life

Whilst scrolling through the photos that I had fa-vourite'd on my phone, I was struck by the varied nature and tone of the photos that I had once fa-vourite'd. A great perspective on life.

13-November-2018

Life is a start, and end.

Life is a duration,
Endured, Enjoyed.

Life is a continuous stream, of stuff.
Life is a series of discrete events.

Life is Boring; Amazing.

Life is unique,
To each person,
To each event.

Life is complicated.

Life is worth it.

Nigel Derbyshire

The wait

For Daisy. As I was waiting to meet a very old friend, it seemed unsettling, familiar, and oddly reassuring.

13-November-2018

Warm golf balls tumble inside,
Familiar and reassuringly unsettling.

Fingers twitch and tap.
Feet ruffle and rock.

Hot palms and,
tingles behind your ears.

Another watchful glance.
Time check. Repeat.

Every noise explored,
Every movement glanced.

Then the Fire of Relief,
On Arrival.

Rich warm smiles.
Hugs.

Calm enjoyments.

Nigel Derbyshire

Golden Spears

---

*Driving back from Town one evening, it was rain-
ing and cold. Then I saw in the distance, the sky
being split by a golden bright line of sunlight.*

26-November-2018

The blazing light of the evening
Pushed the grey clouds to one side.

Its golden spears of bronze light impale
Themselves on my eyes, as I conjure up
The memory of summer warmth.

Distracted and in a non-focused haze,
The grey evening clouds give way to the al-
most-night.

The night enters my head, as the warmth of
Summer fades.

The memory of a warm-summer erased by
the night of the almost-winter.

The cold grey almost-winter, chilling
and inviting.

The strange rush of winter,
separated from the smudge of summer,
by the golden spears of bronze.

Hot Bricks

Whilst waiting to have a mental health assessment, I tried to describe the feeling in my head.

27-November-2018

The sea of hot bricks
in a liquid of saccharin.
Sweet treacle flows
around in my head.

The sharp hot bricks
scuff up against the
raw inside.

I close my eyes to block
out the noise and the
non-physical pain.

Dark blue images dart
into vision, then away.
Help and hope seem so
far away.

Mindful Cornucopia

A warm hand pulls me onto
an island full of strangers.

We are together, safe, unknown.

The bricks move by;
I am no longer at sea.

Nigel Derbyshire

Cambridge

I was in the Baron of Beef pub in Cambridge. Outside in the back, getting some fresh air, drinking a pint of stout and smoking a cigar. A group of young students were there discussing the interviews that they had just had; trying to get into various Cambridge Universities.

I listened for a while, then started to talk to them.

They were raw, full of life and future prospect. I showed them some poetry, followed by an insightful and interesting chat.

The youth of today are so massively underrated. They are full of raw promise and wonder; just waiting to be engaged with.

5-December-2018

Dark Stout
Rich Cigar
Blue Tables.

The Warm Rich Cigar
The Cool Dark Stout
The Light Blue Tables.

Calm.

Ambient chatter of Students
Comparing Notes on Interviews.
Talk of Latin and the Classics.

Water Drips from the Sky,
more chatter about travel without Parents.

The Discussion about Poetry and Writing
Unexpected Completeness.

Nigel Derbyshire

Failure

Bliss is unaware.

Closing

Importance of knowledge that doesn't create wealth

In the beginning...

I had to start somewhere, and it usually starts at the beginning...

As you read that, you will hopefully see it as the cliche that it is supposed to be. Our world is full of cliches.

As I write this I can already feel my eyes glaze over as I attempt to not write another cliche driven piece of writing. Then it occurs to me.

"Is it Saturday today?" - "Yes, all day."

At some singular point in the past, that short phrase was original. Someone somewhere sometime, was the first person to utter those words. It must have been epic. I mean, just think about it for a moment; the first time that came into existence. It must have happened, I mean words don't just appear on their own, someone has to utter them, to write them. There is always a first.

How did it happen? Who was the first person to invent it?

I expect that is something that you have never really considered, except in an inverse kind of way as you inwardly roll your eyes as you hear it for the thousandth time. How did it happen, how did it come into being?

The buzzword here is Knowledge.

It is curious in nature, it is the stuff of the brain, it is something that is intangible but can still be shared. It is something that every human can acquire, and is somehow more than just learning something.

I can learn how to walk, which is more of an instinct thing. However, there is specific knowledge around walking, for example how two legged animals walk differently from four legged animals, that is more than just the learned experience of it. It is something extra. It is knowledge.

Someone learnt how to start a fire, probably by accident; someone had to gain knowledge about

it to allow them to replicate it, and to more effec-
tively pass it onto others.

OK, so knowledge is important. I'm sure you get
that.

In the current material climate that we find ourselves, knowledge good-ness or knowledge bad-
ness is measured by the actions of others and
how they put their knowledge into practice. We
should not encourage the use of knowledge that
leads to people doing bad things.

There is a problem with this social meme. Who
decides. In fact, who decides what potential
knowledge is going to potentially be bad?

We are in an age where people are judged not
just on their actions, but on their potential actions. Furthermore, we are judged on the potential knowledge that we may gain and what we
may do with it that may be bad. That is a lot of
'mays'.

Sure, there are people who set out to do bad
things, from the get-go. Those people have al-

ways existed. They have always been around, and they will always continue to be around.

Sure, there are people who set out to do good things, from the get-go. Those people have always existed. They have always been around, and they will always continue to be around.

In both of those instances, the individuals start with a mind-set or an intent, and pursue knowledge that allows them to get to their end-goal. If you like, the knowledge is gained 'with intent'.

Knowledge-with-intent accounts for the vast majority of the knowledge that humanity has acquired. It is a human trait to want to do something, and then one goes about acquiring the knowledge to make that happen.

There is a subtlety here though. What is actually happening in that situation, is knowledge-copying. The person in question is seeking knowledge and then copying it into their brain. Yes, I know that is odd phrasing, but bear with me.

There is surely a multitude of methods in which the said knowledge can be copied into one's brain, but the key point is that it is copied from 'somewhere'. The knowledge is 'acquired'.

This presents us with somewhat of a complexity, and something that my child brain of yesteryear struggled with. If knowledge is 'acquired' then it must be 'somewhere'. If it is 'somewhere', then it must have got there 'somehow'. If it 'somehow' 'somewhere' then 'how' did it get 'there' ?

You see the problem.

As soon as we start to think of knowledge as a thing, and not a means to a thing, then we start to enter the murky waters of abstraction. Where does knowledge actually come from?

Discovery

Knowledge doesn't just appear out of nowhere, there has to be a unique point of original origin. Or to put it another way, someone has to be first.

This brings me to the main point. The re-purpose of knowledge is everywhere, it is a basic core fabric of all society. It is the basis of re-telling jokes, to the understanding that when we flick a switch that a light will switch on. To say that it is important is more than an understatement.

As I was wandering along the path of this thought experiment, it became so clear that pure knowledge is like gold. Sure, you can make lots of stuff from it, but ultimately someone has to mine it, someone has to discover it.

With something so clearly important, the problem is obvious. In this current society, or version of the world, we attached such status to the 'stuff' that we appear to have overlooked the source material.

Where are the pure knowledge discoverers?

I'm not talking about the knowledge re-purposeers, they are plentiful. No, I am talking about the people who make the discovery of pure knowledge their focus. The people who are not at all interested in what stuff results from the knowledge. The people who are the gold miners.

To say that such people are valuable, would be like saying the surface of the Sun is slightly warm.

Nigel Derbyshire

They are the root of things. Pure knowledge is the root of everything. That much is surely clear.

With something so exciting, one would expect that as a collective we would value those who endeavour to discover pure knowledge; yet we do not. We fear them, we ridicule them, we stop them.

This is surely based on some abstract dotted line that we imagine from the purity of knowledge to the destruction that could be caused by its application. That dotted line is flawed.

For one thing, it assumes that the discoverer is also the applicator. It also implies that knowledge is fundamentally bad unless it can be used for good.

I believe that is also fundamentally flawed.

Pure knowledge is neutral. It has a positive and negative value of zero. Its purity is its value.

Next

With something so valuable at stake and at such short supply, we should be proactively provoking its discovery.

Knowledge can be used to do good things, it can be used to do bad things. One thing is sure though, without pure-root-knowledge we are doomed.

Proactively empower those who are able to discover pure-root-knowledge. We should support them, we should give them all the tools they need. We should never measure any "success" from them; that is an outcome and they do not create outcomes.

We should protect them; we should love them. For if we do not, we are doomed to an ever decreasing and ever diminishing circle of recycling.

Nigel Derbyshire

About the author

Nigel Derbyshire grew up in Norfolk, is well travelled and now lives in Cambridgeshire.

An eater of cheese, drinker of red wine and ale, he is a reformed lover of people and conversation. Always adventuring into the textures of life, Nigel occasionally remembers to write some of it down.

Crafting dense free verse poetry, Nigel meanders the boundaries between his internal reality and the external perception of reality.

Not as scary as he sounds; feel free to connect via

twitter   -   @carbonwriter

or

email   -   nigel@carbonwriter.net

nigelderbyshire.com